Dear Parents:

Congratulations! Your child is taking the first steps on an exciting journey. The destination? Independent reading!

STEP INTO READING® will help your child get there. The program offers five steps to reading success. Each step includes fun stories and colorful art or photographs. In addition to original fiction and books with favorite characters, there are Step into Reading Non-Fiction Readers, Phonics Readers and Boxed Sets, Sticker Readers, and Comic Readers—a complete literacy program with something to interest every child.

Learning to Read, Step by Step!

Ready to Read Preschool–Kindergarten
• big type and easy words • rhyme and rhythm • picture clues
For children who know the alphabet and are eager to begin reading.

Reading with Help Preschool–Grade 1
• basic vocabulary • short sentences • simple stories
For children who recognize familiar words and sound out new words with help.

Reading on Your Own Grades 1–3
• engaging characters • easy-to-follow plots • popular topics
For children who are ready to read on their own.

Reading Paragraphs Grades 2–3
• challenging vocabulary • short paragraphs • exciting stories
For newly independent readers who read simple sentences with confidence.

Ready for Chapters Grades 2–4
• chapters • longer paragraphs • full-color art
For children who want to take the plunge into chapter books but still like colorful pictures.

STEP INTO READING® is designed to give every child a successful reading experience. The grade levels are only guides; children will progress through the steps at their own speed, developing confidence in their reading.

Remember, a lifetime love of reading starts with a single step!

Special thanks to Venetia Davie, Ryan Ferguson, Charnita Belcher, Tanya Mann, Julia Phelps, Sharon Woloszyk, Nicole Corse, Darren Sander, Rita Lichtwardt, Debra Zakarin, Karen Painter, Stuart Smith, Carla Alford, Julia Pistor, Renata Marchand, Michelle Cogan, Shareena Carlson, Kris Fogel, Rainmaker Entertainment and Conrad Helten and Lilian Bravo

Published in the United States by Random House Children's Books, a division of Penguin Random House LLC, 1745 Broadway, New York, NY 10019, and in Canada by Random House of Canada, a division of Penguin Random House Ltd., Toronto.

Step into Reading, Random House, and the Random House colophon are registered trademarks of Penguin Random House LLC.

Visit us on the Web!
StepIntoReading.com
randomhousekids.com

Educators and librarians, for a variety of teaching tools, visit us at RHTeachersLibrarians.com

ISBN 978-1-101-93140-0 (trade) — ISBN 978-1-101-93141-7 (lib. bdg.) — ISBN 978-1-101-93142-4 (ebook)

Printed in the United States of America
12 11 10 9 8

Random House Children's Books supports the First Amendment and celebrates the right to read.

STEP INTO READING®

Barbie SPY SQUAD

SUPER AGENTS

Adapted by Melissa Lagonegro

Based on the screenplay by
Marsha Griffin and Kacey Arnold

Illustrated by Ulkutay Design Group

Random House 🏠 New York

Barbie, Renee, and Teresa
are great gymnasts.
They practice.

Renee's auntie Zoe loves
to watch the girls
compete as a team.

The girls go
to meet Auntie Zoe.
A secret door opens.

They find
a secret agency!
Auntie Zoe is in charge.
She wants the girls
to help find a gem thief.

The girls meet two agents.
Lazslo gives them spy gear.
They get robot pets!

Agent Dunbar will
train them.

The girls start training.
They climb walls.
They flip and jump
over laser beams.
They must work together!

The spy squad is ready
for its first mission!

Barbie spots
the thief.
The thief
steals a jewel
and gets away!

The spy squad wears
disguises for the
next mission.

The thief does
a triple flip.
The thief gets away
with a gem!

At practice,

Patricia does a triple flip.

Patricia is the thief!

She gets away again.

The girls follow Patricia
to the agency.

She is working
with Agent Dunbar!
They have all the gems!
Dunbar's robots capture
Barbie and her friends.

Patricia changes
her mind.
She helps Barbie.

Barbie uses a super kick.

She knocks Dunbar down!

Dunbar is trapped!
Auntie Zoe arrives.

She is proud of the girls.

Their job is not done.

They must get the gems

out of a dangerous device!

Renee and Teresa
help Barbie.
She gets a gem out.
The girls work together
to destroy the device.

Patricia is happy

to be part

of a new team.

Barbie, Renee, and Teresa
win their competition.
Together, they can do
anything!

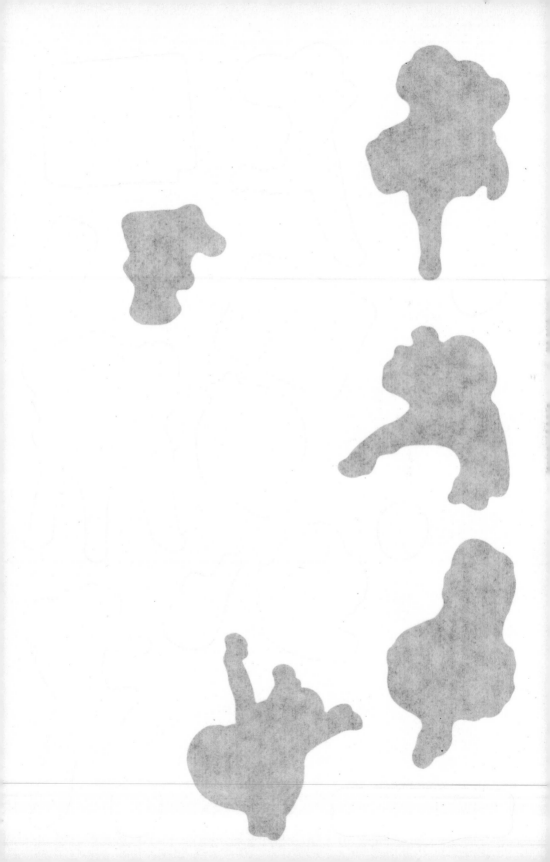